DINOSAURS!

STRANGE AND WONDERFUL

by LAURENCE PRINGLE   *Illustrated by* CAROL HEYER

BOYDS MILLS PRESS

Stegoceras (steg-OSS-air-us)

For Margaret K. McElderry, *who in 1967 accepted my first book manuscript—about dinosaurs—after it had been rejected by eight other editors* —L.P.

For my parents and mentors,
William J. Heyer *and*
Merlyn M. Heyer,
now and always —C.H.

Text copyright © 1995 by Laurence Pringle
Illustrations copyright © 1995 by Carol Heyer

Published by Caroline House
Boyds Mills Press, Inc.
A Highlights Company
815 Church Street
Honesdale, Pennsylvania 18431
Printed in USA

Publisher Cataloging-in-Publication Data
Pringle, Laurence.
   Dinosaurs! : strange and wonderful / by Laurence Pringle ; illustrated
by Carol Heyer.—1st ed.
[32]p. : col. ill. ; cm.
Summary : Dramatic, accurate illustrations accompany basic facts about
dinosaurs.
ISBN 1-878093-16-9
1. Dinosaurs—Juvenile literature. 2. Paleontology—Juvenile literature.
[1. Dinosaurs. 2. Paleontology.] I. Heyer, Carol, ill. II. Title.
567.9'1—dc20   1995   CIP
Library of Congress Catalog Card Number 92-71273

First edition, 1995
Book designed by Joy Chu
The text of this book is set in 20-point Times Roman.
The illustrations are done in acrylics.
Distributed by St. Martin's Press

10 9 8 7 6 5 4 3 2

The author thanks Peter Dodson, Ph.D., professor of anatomy at the
School of Veterinary Medicine and adjunct professor of geology at the
University of Pennsylvania in Philadelphia, for reviewing the text and
illustrations of this book for accuracy.

CLOSE YOUR EYES,

and imagine a time —
long, long ago —when there
were no people on earth.
There were also no cats or dogs,
no cows, no zebras,
no elephants.

Imagine that dinosaurs lived almost everywhere on land.
They lived in green forests and brown deserts.

Struthiomimus (STRU-thee-o-MY-mus)

Troödon (TROO-o-don)

They lived in soggy swamps and on windswept prairies.

Edmontosaurus (ed-MON-tuh-SAW-rus)

Parasaurolophus (PAIR-ah-saw-ROL-o-fuss)

Dinosaurs may have walked where you live. Imagine that! But dinosaurs were not make-believe. They were real animals that lived in a time we call the Age of Reptiles.

In that time, large reptiles soared in the sky. Giant swimming reptiles chased fish in the seas. And dinosaurs ruled the land.

Pteranodon (ter-RAN-o-don), a pterosaur (not a dinosaur)

We learn about dinosaurs and other living things of long ago from clues, called fossils, preserved in rocks. Most fossils are bones and teeth. Sometimes all of the bones of an animal's skeleton are discovered. Other times only a few bones are found.

The people who study fossils are called paleontologists (PAY-lee-on-TOL-o-jists). They have learned a lot about the dinosaurs that lived millions of years ago.

More than three hundred kinds of dinosaurs have been identified and given special names by paleontologists. These names come from Greek or Latin words. They sound strange at first.

One dinosaur is called *Triceratops* (tri-SAIR-ah-tops). This name means "three-horn face." Three big horns stuck out from the head of this plant-eating dinosaur.

Another dinosaur was *Velociraptor* (vuh-LOSS-ah-RAP-tor), which means "swift one that seizes prey." A speedy hunter, *Velociraptor* was about the size of a wolf.

Protoceratops (PRO-toe-SAIR-uh-tops) under attack

Stegosaurus (STEG-uh-SAW-rus) was a plant-eating dinosaur as long as two automobiles. Its name means "covered lizard."

Big, flat bony plates have been found with its fossil bones and teeth. People have wondered where the plates fit on the body of *Stegosaurus*. Were they stuck on the dinosaur's sides, like armor? Did they somehow fit in an upright pattern along its backbone?

Today many paleontologists believe that the plates grew as they are shown on the *Stegosaurus* at the top right.

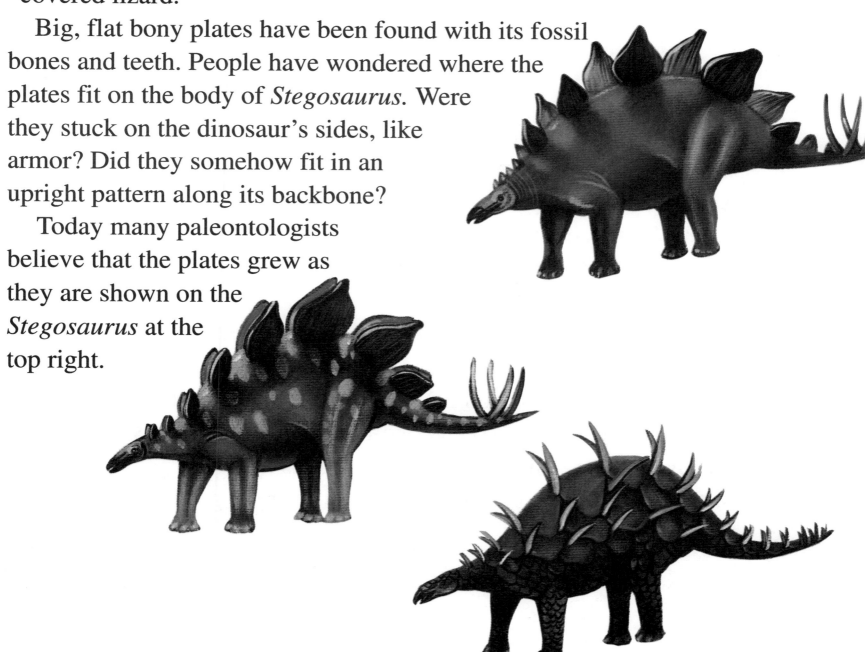

Some dinosaurs were giants. Those known as sauropods (SAW-ruh-pods) were the biggest animals that ever lived on land.

Brachiosaurus (BRACK-ee-uh-SAW-rus), or "arm lizard," was one sauropod. From nose to tail its body stretched as long as two big school buses.

Apatosaurus (ah-PAT-uh-SAW-rus), or "deceptive lizard," was another sauropod. It used to be called *Brontosaurus* (BRON-tuh-SAW-rus), or "thunder lizard." With giant feet, each two and one-half feet long, perhaps *Apatosaurus* and all of the other sauropods made a thunderous noise as they walked or ran over the ground.

Brachiosaurus (BRACK-ee-uh-SAW-rus)

Huge bones of other sauropods have been dug from the earth. Parts of a *Seismosaurus* (SIZE-mo-SAW-rus) skeleton were found in New Mexico.

One shoulder bone found in Colorado measures nine feet long. It is the largest dinosaur bone ever discovered. This bone was once part of a sauropod named *Ultrasaurus* (UL-tra-SAW-rows).

Only a few bones of *Ultrasaurus* and other very large sauropods have been found. These dinosaurs were taller than four elephants. If more of their skeleton parts are found, we can learn more about the lives of these mysterious giants.

Lexovisaurus (lex-OH-vee-SAW-rus) in background

For every big sauropod there were many dinosaurs the size of horses, giraffes, ostriches, and dogs. The smallest known dinosaur is *Compsognathus* (KOMP-sog-NAY-thus). It was the size and shape of a skinny chicken, about two feet long.

Compsognathus did not peck at seeds for its food. Instead it raced after swift lizards and gobbled them down. A paleontologist found the bones of a lizard among the ribs of a *Compsognathus* skeleton. The lizard may have been the little dinosaur's last meal.

The word dinosaur means "terrible lizard," but dinosaurs were not lizards, and most of them were peaceful plant eaters. By looking at their jaws and teeth, paleontologists can tell that some dinosaurs ate soft fruits and leaves. Others nibbled on buds and twigs from trees.

Apatosaurus (ah-PAT-uh-SAW-rus)

A few dinosaurs had sharp, pointed teeth. They had claws for grabbing and ripping. These dinosaurs hunted other creatures for their food.

Deinonychus (dine-ON-ik-us)

Allosaurus (AL-uh-SAW-rus) was a mighty hunter. Its body and tail together were as long as a big school bus. But one *Allosaurus* could not bring down a huge sauropod. *Allosaurus* may have hunted in packs.

Plant-eating dinosaurs defended themselves from attack. Adult sauropods may have formed a circle around their young to keep them safe.

Baby dinosaurs hatched from eggs. As many as twenty-five dinosaur eggs have been found in one nest.

One duck-billed dinosaur was given the name *Maiasaura* (MY-ah-SAW-ruh), which means "good mother lizard." *Maiasaura* mothers made round nests of mud in which they laid their eggs. The nests were about the size of your bed. They brought plant food to the nests until their young were big enough to take care of themselves.

Each year paleontologists dig new fossils from the ground and learn more about dinosaurs. Many new kinds of dinosaurs have been found in China, Australia, Argentina, Mongolia, and North America.

In Montana, more fossil bones of *Tyrannosaurus* (tye-RAN-uh-SAW-rus) have been discovered. The front legs of this mighty hunter were once thought to be weak. Study of newly found bones shows that *Tyrannosaurus* had big muscles on its short arms. Each arm was probably strong enough to lift your mother and father!

From fossils we have learned a lot about dinosaurs and how they lived. But fossils do not show the color of dinosaurs, or the sounds they made.

Perhaps dinosaurs had patterns of colors like those of lizards and other reptiles living today.

Did some dinosaurs roar and bellow? Did they whoop or whistle? The sounds that dinosaurs made will always be a mystery.

Pachyrhinosaurus (PAK-ee-RYE-no-SAW-rus)

One of the greatest of all mysteries is why the
dinosaurs died out. The last of the dinosaurs died
65 million years ago. So did the flying reptiles and
the large reptiles of the seas.

Some paleontologists believe that a few kinds of small dinosaurs may have survived. They changed over a period of millions of years. Today we call them birds.

Ornithomimids (or-NITH-o-MY-mids)

ONLY SOME FOOTPRINTS, bones, and other fossils are left to tell us about dinosaurs. As we find more of these clues, we may learn why the dinosaurs died out. We will also learn more about the lives of these amazing animals that walked the earth for 160 million years.